LITTLE FOX, lost

Nicole Snitselaar • Alicia Padrón

Translated from French by Erin Woods

pajamapress

First published in the United States and Canada in 2016
Text copyright © 2016 Nicole Snitselaar
Illustration copyright © 2016 Alicia Padrón
This edition copyright © 2016 Pajama Press Inc.
Translated from the French by Erin Woods
Originally published in French by éditions Les 400 coups.

10 9 8 7 6 5 4 3 2 1

The publisher gratefully acknowledges the support of the Canada Council for the Arts and the Ontario Arts Council for its publishing program. We acknowledge the financial support of the Government of Canada through the Canada Book Fund (CBF) for our publishing activities.

Library and Archives Canada Cataloguing in Publication
Snitselaar, Nicole, 1956- [Petit renard se perd. English]
Little fox, lost / Nicole Snitselaar ; [illustrated by] Alicia Padrón
; translated from French by Erin Woods.
Translation of: Petit renard se perd. ISBN 978-1-77278-004-8 (hardback)
I. Padron, Alicia, illustrator II. Woods, Erin, 1989-, translator
III. Title. IV. Title: Petit renard se perd. English.
PZ7.S6785Li 2016   j843'.92   C2016-901451-

Publisher Cataloging-in-Publication Data (U.S.)
Names: Snitselaar, Nicole, author. | Padron, Alicia, illustrator. | Woods, Erin, translator.
Title: Little Fox, lost / Nicole Snitselaar, Alicia Padron ; translated from French by Erin Woods.
Description: Toronto, Ontario Canada : Pajama Press, 2016. | Originally published in French by Éditions Les 400 coups, Montreal, Canada, as Petit renard se perd. | Summary: "Little Fox is lost in the snowy forest. When an old owl offers to help him find his way home, Little Fox remembers his mother's rhyming warning to stay still if he is lost. Instead of following a stranger, Little Fox finds a better solution: He lets the other animals help him sing his mother's rhyme until she follows their voices to him"— Provided by publisher.
Identifiers: ISBN 978-1-77278-004-8 (hardcover)
Subjects: LCSH: Strangers – Juvenile fiction. | Foxes – Juvenile fiction. | Mother and child—Juvenile fiction. | Obedience – Juvenile fiction. | BISAC: JUVENILE FICTION / Social Themes / Strangers. | JUVENILE FICTION / Animals / Foxes. | JUVENILE FICTION / Family / Parents.
Classification: LCC PZ7.S658Lit |DDC [E] – dc23

Manufactured by Transcontinental Printing
Printed in Canada

Pajama Press Inc.
181 Carlaw Ave. Suite 207 Toronto, Ontario Canada, M4M 2S1

Distributed in Canada by UTP Distribution
5201 Dufferin Street Toronto, Ontario Canada, M3H 5T8

Distributed in the U.S. by Ingram Publisher Services
1 Ingram Blvd. La Vergne, TN 37086, USA

It had snowed all morning,
and now the sun was showing its face at last.
Everything was sparkling and white.

"Shall we go walking?"
asked Mama Fox.

"Oh, yes!" cried Little Fox.
He loved to play in the snow.

"Stay close," Mama Fox reminded him. "You don't want to get lost."

Down the path, Mama Fox met
Mrs. Gray Fox.
"Isn't it a lovely day?" The two of
them began to chat.

It didn't take long for Little Fox to
get bored. He decided to find some
fun of his own.

"If I take ten steps ahead,
three behind,
six to the right,
and two to the left,
Where will I end up?" he wondered.

Little Fox looked over his shoulder.
His paw prints had made pictures
in the snow.

"If I go 'round this tree,
under that branch,
and over the little bridge...
If I run very fast...
What will my tracks look like then?"

As he spoke, Little Fox skipped away.
He didn't realize he was running deeper
and deeper into the forest.

*S*uddenly, Little Fox stopped short.
He couldn't see Mama Fox anywhere.
"Where am I? How did I get here?"

He looked around. His paw prints ran
in every direction.
How could he ever retrace his steps?

"Mama! I'm lost!"
Little Fox was afraid. He began to cry.

"Don't be frightened," rumbled
a deep voice.
Startled, Little Fox looked up to see
an old owl sitting on a branch.

"I'm not allowed to talk to people
I don't know," Little Fox hiccupped
between two sobs.

"Don't be frightened," Old Owl said again.
"I can fly high in the air, and I can see far ahead.
I will take you back to your mother. Follow me!"
Old Owl set off, swooping between the trees.
Little Fox raced after him.

Then he stopped.

"No! I can't!"

"You can't what?" asked Old Owl.
"I can't follow you," said Little Fox. "I've just
remembered what Mama always says:

'If ever you are lost, my child,
Don't let a stranger guide you.
Be still, and I will search the wild
Until I am beside you.'"

"Well," Old Owl grumbled. "If that's what your Mama says, then I guess you'd better listen to her. You are lost, so sit still and wait right there."

And that's just what Little Fox did.

Several long minutes passed.
Then Little Fox said, "I have a good idea! If we sing Mama's rhyme together, she might hear us."

And so Little Fox and Old Owl began to sing.
Little by little, other forest animals drew closer.
They began to join the song...

"If ever you are lost, my child,
Don't let a stranger guide you.
Be still, and I will search the wild
Until I am beside you."

Soon, Mama Fox came running through the trees, all out of breath.
"Little Fox! I've been searching everywhere!"

Oh, Mama, I was so afraid!" Little Fox sniffed.
"It's all my fault. I'm sorry I wandered off."

Mama Fox led the way home.
She was proud of her Little Fox.
He had done exactly what he should.

That night, safe in his den,
Little Fox fell asleep with the words
of Mama's song playing in his head:

"If ever you are lost, my child,
Don't let a stranger guide you.
Be still, and I will search the wild
Until I am beside you."